Robert Quackenbush
LOST IN THE AMAZON
A Miss Mallard Mystery

Pippin Press
New York

Published by Pippin Press, 229 East 85th Street
Gracie Station Box 92
New York, N.Y. 10028

Printed in the United States of America
by Horowitz/Rae Book Manufacturers, Inc.

10 9 8 7 6 5 4 3 2 1

Library of Congress Cataloging-in-Publication Data

Library of Congress Cataloging-in-Publication Data

Quackenbush, Robert M.
  Lost in the Amazon

    Summary: When a brilliant scientist is abducted
from a hotel in Rio de Janeiro, Miss Mallard, the
famous ducktective, embarks on a dangerous search
that takes her deep into the Amazon jungle.
    [1. Mystery and detective stories. 2. Ducks—
Fiction. 3. Jungles—Fiction. 4. Brazil—Fiction]
I. Title.
PZ7.Q16Lo 1990 [E]   90-7524
ISBN 0-945912-11-0

Miss Mallard, the world-famous ducktective, flew to Rio de Janeiro, Brazil at carnival time. It so happened that an old friend, Dr. Albert Eiderstein, the great European scientist, was there at the same time. He came to Rio to be honored at a press luncheon, where he planned to announce his latest discovery. He sent Miss Mallard an invitation and a program especially autographed to her, with a beautiful butterfly drawn below his name.

In the hotel dining room, everyone was quacking with excitement. Then a hush fell as Dr. Eiderstein took his place at the speaker's platform. Standing next to him was Miguel de Duckerio, who was president of duckdom's Save the Amazon Rain Forest Society, better known as SARF.

Without saying a word, the genius of science poured a few drops of liquid from a tiny vial onto a dying plant. At once the plant sprung to life, grew tall and flowered. The surprised audience burst into a thunderous applause.

Dr. Eiderstein put the vial next to the plant. Then he held up his wings and stopped all the noise and clapping.

"I call my discovery Jungle-Nu," he said. "The message is clear: SAVE THE AMAZON RAIN FOREST. Every year millions of acres of trees are slashed and burned by ranchers and builders. They are bent on clearing the jungle to make way for crops, cattle pastures, electric-power dams and gold mines. In a few years the jungle will become a desert wasteland. Gone will be the home for millions of plants and animals. A species a day is being destroyed. ACT NOW! Restore the damage with Jungle-Nu. Then allow scientists time for careful study to find ways to use the jungle without disturbing its natural wonders."

"Phooey!" quacked Jorge Baldpate, a rancher. "Your idea stinks."

"It will never work," quacked Lenos Ruddy Duck, a miner. "Stop wasting our time."

"It's all done with mirrors," quacked Vasco Scoter, a planter.

Suddenly there was a loud commotion. A parade of samba dancers burst into the dining room. They danced and chanted as they wove snake-fashion in between the tables. Such a racket! Then, as quickly as they came in, they all left. Afterwards, everyone realized that something terrible had happened during the confusion. Dr. Eiderstein was swept away and so was his vial of Jungle-Nu!

"Follow the dancers!" someone quacked.

The waiters ran outside, but the dancers were gone. The manager called the police and a team of squad cars came skidding up to the hotel. Inspector Alfonso Buffle-Head was in charge of the investigation. He spotted Miss Mallard.

"I'm glad to know that a ducktective of your reputation is visiting Brazil," he said. "I may need you later."

Inspector Buffle-Head checked Dr. Eiderstein's room. It was empty except for an unsigned note in a wastebasket. The note threatened Dr. Eiderstein with harm unless he left Brazil immediately.

Inspector Buffle-Head was baffled. He showed the note to Miss Mallard.

"I need your help sooner than I thought," he said.

"I'll begin now," said Miss Mallard.

First she asked Miguel de Duckerio what he had seen since he stood next to Dr. Eiderstein at the speaker's platform.

"I saw nothing," he said. "I was in the hall making a phone call while Dr. Eiderstein was speaking. When I returned he was gone and so was his vial of Jungle-Nu."

Miss Mallard looked into the hall outside the dining room. Sure enough, there were two pay phones. One was out of order, but the other was not.

Next, Miss Mallard went outside to see if there were any witnesses when the samba dancers left the hotel.

A volunteer for SARF, who was handing out leaflets, had some information.

"I saw a dancer in a straw costume and a duck in a white suit leave in a taxi," said the volunteer. "The driver was told to go to the small airport north of the city."

"I remember that dancer!" exclaimed Miss Mallard. "And the duck in white would be Dr. Eiderstein! I must rush to the airport!"

She thanked the volunteer and took a leaflet. She glanced at it. She saw a list of members. She was puzzled. The list included Vasco Scoter, Lenos Ruddy Duck, and Jorge Baldpate. She remembered how they protested Dr. Eiderstein's discovery. She shook her head and quickly hailed a taxi.

On the way to the airport, Miss Mallard had a talkative driver. He knew a lot about Rio. She asked him if he had heard of Vasco Scoter, Lenos Ruddy Duck, and Jorge Baldpate.

"They are in the news a lot," he said. "They join worthwhile societies that make them look good. But I heard that they own jungle land that they are clearing to make money."

"Hmm," said Miss Mallard.

At the airport terminal, a
pilot told Miss Mallard that, yes,
the two ducks she described had
been there. A private jet flew
them to an unknown destination.

Miss Mallard looked at a map
of the Amazon basin on the wall.
It was marked with symbols to
show runways in the jungle. One
runway had a butterfly symbol with
the words *Ze-Ze Quacken*.

"Hmm," said Miss Mallard aloud.
"Where have I seen that before?"

She remembered. She reached in
her knitting bag for the program
Dr. Eiderstein had autographed. She
opened it to the page he had signed.

"Ah, ha!" she said. "Here is the
same symbol below Dr. Eiderstein's
signature. He drew it himself."

She got an idea. She called
Inspector Buffle-Head and arranged
for a pilot and a private jet.

"I want to go to Ze-Ze Quacken,"
she said.

Within a few hours, the pilot landed his jet on the Ze-Ze Quacken runway. He handed Miss Mallard a net for her hat to protect her face from insects and pointed to a river.

"That's the Rio de Shivers," he said. "It is one of the mighty Amazon's many tributaries. You'll find a raft on the bank. Take it downstream until you come to an Indian village —the home of the Ze-Ze Quacken tribe. That is the nearest settlement."

"Come back for me tomorrow," said Miss Mallard.

With that, the pilot flew off and Miss Mallard stood alone on the runway. She listened. Everything was quiet. Too quiet. All at once she heard buzzing, hissing, squawking, and chattering noises coming from the jungle around her. Then she heard an awful shriek followed by a mournful wail that sent shivers down her spine.

In a flash, she ran to the river. She grabbed an oar and headed downstream on the raft as fast as she could.

As Miss Mallard guided her raft
on the river, a black cloud of
zillions of flies, gnats, and
mosquitoes stormed over her head.
She was grateful for the net the
pilot had given her.

She began to worry. Could she
survive the river's rapids, piranhas,
and two hundred foot water snakes
that she knew lurked there?

"Stop that, Margery Mallard!" she
quacked to herself. "Worrisome thoughts
are a hindrance! You have a job to do!"

She bravely kept her raft on a
steady course. Before long, she came
to a place where the river branched
out in two directions. She wondered
which way to go—left or right?

Then she saw a bit of straw floating
next to the bank at her right, like
the straw on the samba dancer's costume.

"Right is right," she said aloud.
"I know it, the same way I know that
crime does not pay."

As she rounded the bend, Miss Mallard felt her raft being pulled. She was caught in a whirlpool!

She scrabbled at the water with her oar to slow the dizzy spinning. Time after time she fought toward the edge of the whirlpool only to be pulled back. Blinded by sweat, the strength ebbing from her wings, she felt the raft lurch closer and closer to being swallowed up.

Slowly, slowly she worked to get beyond the ring of foam. But it was hopeless. Then she saw a tree branch overhead. She tossed her pole in the water, picked up her knitting bag, and grabbed hold of the branch just as the raft was being sucked out from under her.

Wing over wing, she worked her way along the branch until she was clear of the whirlpool. She saw a giant lily pad drifting toward her. She let go of the branch and landed on the pad. Grabbing her pole as it came floating by, she proceeded on her journey.

At last Miss Mallard came to
the village of the Ze-Ze Quacken
tribe. A group of Indian ducks
came to meet her. The samba dancer
was among them. The group stepped
aside to let someone through. Miss
Mallard knew at once who it was.

"Dr. Eiderstein, I presume,"
said Miss Mallard.

They hugged one another like long
lost ducks do when they have passed
through a terrible ordeal.

Dr. Eiderstein said, "I trusted
only you, Margery, with the knowledge
of my hiding place. That is why I
sketched the butterfly symbol next
to my signature in your program.
But I didn't dream that you would
come all this way to seek me out."

"I had to know that you were
safe," said Miss Mallard. "But
why did you leave Rio?"

"I had no other choice," said
Dr. Eiderstein. "My lab papers
were stolen from my room and I
had received threats."

The samba dancer stepped forward.

"Meet my adopted son, Ura-Eu," said Dr. Eiderstein. "I found him years ago when I made my first expedition to the Amazon. I took him to Europe and trained him to work with me. We planned my escape."

Ura-Eu spoke up and said, "I hired dancers and dressed in my native costume so no one would recognize me. While everyone was being distracted, Dad ran to his room, grabbed his suitcase, and met me outside. The rest you know."

"All for nothing," said Dr. Eiderstein. "With my papers gone, my only hope was the vial of Jungle-Nu. I planned to analyze the contents and restore the formula. But when I reached for it as I fled the dining room, it was gone!"

All at once everything became clear to Miss Mallard.

"I think I know where to find the vial!" she said. "Help me to get back to Rio and I'll send it to you!"

Miss Mallard stayed overnight
at the village. At dawn she set
off with Ura-Eu as her guide through
the jungle to the runway. The pilot
was waiting for her and they flew off.

When she arrived at the hotel,
Miss Mallard freshened up. Afterwards,
she went over every detail of the
case. Then she called Inspector
Buffle-Head for a meeting outside the
dining room. He was to bring along
Jorge Baldpate, Lenos Ruddy Duck,
Vasco Scoter, and Miguel de Duckerio.

As soon as everyone was assembled,
Miss Mallard told them about Dr.
Eiderstein and how he needed the vial.

"But the vial is missing," said
Inspector Buffle-Head.

"Not true," said Miss Mallard.

She opened the coin return slot of
the broken pay phone. She reached inside
and pulled out the vial with a hanky
to preserve tell-tale prints.

Everyone gasped. Miguel de Duckerio
started to leave.

"Freeze!" said Inspector Buffle-Head.

Miguel de Duckerio stayed put.

Miss Mallard said to him, "Confess! You hid the vial in the out-of-order pay phone—a place you thought would not be discovered. You did it while Dr. Eiderstein was making his speech. Your motive was payoff money. Certain members of SARF gave it to you so you would approve the clearing of jungle land for their profit-making schemes."

She held up the SARF leaflet.

"Their names appear on this leaflet: Jorge Baldpate, Lenos Ruddy Duck, and Vasco Scoter."

"You idiot, Miguel!" quacked Vasco.

"Yeah!" quacked Lenos. "You told us you would destroy that vial!"

"The same way you destroyed Eiderstein's lab papers that you stole," quacked Jorge.

Miguel said meekly, "I forgot to come back for it. You had me doing too much."

Inspector Buffle-Head had heard enough. He arrested all four and took them to jail.

"Thanks to you, Miss Mallard," he said, "this case is closed."

"It was thrilling," said Miss Mallard. "Every minute of it."

She said goodbye and went to her room. She wrapped the vial of Jungle-Nu for mailing to Dr. Eiderstein. Then she packed for her return flight to London.

At the airport, a crowd of grateful Brazilians came to see her off. They made speeches and sang songs about her. Then they appointed her the new president and world-wide representative of SARF.

"I am very honored," said Miss Mallard. "I will spread the good word about the society wherever I go. I will answer letters from concerned ducks and pass their solutions for saving the rain forest on to Dr. Eiderstein."

With that she threw them all a kiss and danced the samba up the steps and into the plane.